Who am I,
if not a collector
of the vanished gaze?

Zrze, Macedonia, June 2001

Roger Colombik
A Quiet Divide

Plain View Press
P O 42255
Austin, TX 78704

plainviewpress.net
sbright1@austin.rr.com
1-512-441-2452

Roger Colombik

A Quiet Divide

For Jerry: Heart & Soul, Patience & Understanding

Special Thanks —

Flori & Sasho Boskovski who took Jerry and I back in time into the heartland of Macedonia, Dr. Ivan Dejanov and Dr. Samuel Sadikario for sharing their dream of remembrance, Radu & Liliana Moraru who always welcome us with open arms, Serhiy Proskurnia for humor and enlightenment, Matei Benjanaru for introducing me to East European Conceptualism and then trying to explain it, Georgeta Cazacu who never flinched when I would point out a street person to interview, Dushan & Agnes Petrovic for outstanding Serbian hospitality, Justus Weiner for his kindness and encyclopedic mind on the Middle East, Maxim Dumitras and the fabled characters of Singeorz-Bai, Greddy Assa who welcomed me with open arms, The Center For Polish Sculpture, Struga Poetry Evenings, the International Symposium in Prilep, Texas State University - San Marcos Research Enhancement Program, the sculptors of Bulgaria who welcomed me with wine and stories, Rudolf Kocsis and his grandfather's brandy, Alexander and Natalia Hadjiivanov for their warmth and humor, the students in Cluj, Timisoara, Iasi, and Sofia who taught me so much, to the many, many people who opened their doors and hearts to a stranger, Susan Bright for her patience and guidance. And a special thanks to the gentleman who had chutzpah to approach us on a train and ascertain, "Your Americans, right. Good. Can I ask you a question. Good. Do you mind talking politics? Great. How come the US supports Albanian terrorists?"

Contents

Prologue   14

Adrift   17

Adrift   18
Arrival   19
Zamosc   20
The Firmament of Neglect   21
The Horseman   24
Two Women   25
Fifteen Years   26
Journal Notes   27
The Frontier   28
A Band of Gypsies   30
For Luminista   31
Conversation on a Park Bench   32

Christmas in Bethlehem   35

Hitchhiking in the West Bank I   40
First Impressions: The City of David   41
Journal Notes   42
Journal Notes   43
Gideon   44
Jerusalem '93   45
Christmas in Bethlehem   46
Journal Notes: Interview with Ali Jeddah   48
Crayons   49
Journal Notes   50
Ramallah Redux   52
Hitchhiking in the West Bank II   53

A Quiet Divide   55

Return to the Land of Alexander   58
A Day in the Life of Father Kliment   60
The Call to Arms   62

Violeta   63
Channel Surfing   64
Vevchani: Excerpts From Market Day, July 2001   65
In Memory of Dr. Dejanov   66
For Dushan   68
Belgrade Street Corner   70
77 Nights: A Bedtime Rhyme   71
Balkan Express   72
The Nightly News   73
First Impressions: Albania   74
Last Thoughts On Macedonia   77

Ground Cover   79

The Persistence of Memory   82
Footprints   83
Homecoming   86
Eternal Grey   87

Balkan Summer   91

Balkan Summer   92
Singeorz-Bai   94
Tonel Schlessinger and the Jews of Arad, Romania   96
Forty Years   100
Journal Notes: Robert Bly For A Day   101
St. Marko   104
Monastir   106
Departure   107

About the Author   112

Photographs

Zrze, Macedonia, June 2001   2
Jerry in Safronbolou, Turkey, 1996   8
Buraj Ramadan   15
The Horseman, Iasi, Romania, 2001   22
The Romanian Frontier, 2001   28
For Luminitsa   31
Emerich, August 3, 2001   32
Bethlehem Storefront, Dec. 24, 1995   36
Families on their way to the Nativity, Bethlehem, Dec. 23, 1995 38
The City of David   41
Bethlehem Square, Dec. 23, 1995   47
East Jerusalem, June, 1993   50
Kishtani, Macedonia, July 2001   56
Violeta Yovanoska   63
TV War Coverage, Prilep, Macedonia, June, 2001   64
Milam Petrovic, Belgrade, 2001   69
Hungarian Countryside, 1998   72
Struga, Macedonia, August, 1998   75
Albanian bride, Struga Macedonia, July, 2001   76
New Jewish Cemetery, Krakow, Poland, 1993   80
Kazmierz Dolny, Poland, 1993   84
Janowiec, Poland, 1993   88
Singeorz-Bai, Romania, 2001   93
Singeorz-Bai, Romania, 2001   95
Maria, Vitolishte, Macedonia, 1998   98
Struga Poetry Evenings, Macedonia, 1998   102
St. Marko, Prilep, Macedonia, 1998   104
Monastir, Bulgaria, June 13, 2001   106
Ancient Croatian Manuscript, Rijeka, Croatia   108
Constantine's Father, Putna, Romania   110

Prologue

The train car is sweltering and the open window provides scant relief from the searing afternoon heat. The station platform is overflowing with families and the cacophonous screaming of children. An immense man appears in the doorway of our cabin with pleading eyes. No words are necessary. We quickly rearrange the space in order to accommodate the kids. Three young boys in matching outfits race towards the window. The mother stumbles in and collapses onto the seat with a rambunctious infant in her arms. She thanks us for the cabin but she is especially grateful for the bottle of aspirin we hand her. The father strikes up a conversation of family holidays and refuge from the chaos in the south. He takes a long drag on his cigarette and mutters something about K4 and the UN. The eldest child decides to sweat out the ride in the cramped corridor. The two little ones joyfully immerse themselves in a snack. And one child appears content to sit out the journey, quietly staring into the eyes of a stranger.

Buraj, son of Ramadan Demirovic, Serbia

Adrift

Journal Notes

What does it mean to be a drifter
In a country already adrift?

Hitchhiking with Gypsies
Samakov, Bulgaria, June 5, 2001

Arrival

Skinny children play
in murky pools of water
Along railroad tracks
they'll never travel

~

A solitary figure
upon a mountain
of burning trash
Biblical premonitions
far removed
from the holy land

~

A welcome committee of children
Arms raised high
in blissful exaltation
floats past as I disembark
Flying on fumes
of plastic bag inhalers
A treacherous dance
of leaden paint highs

Zamosc

New Year's Eve
with nothin' but sardines and vodka
to close out the night
as empty shelves stare back at disbelieving eyes.
But with the butcher in high spirits
and a round of drinks for all
social inequities and queues for food seem to disappear
in this post-communist/still communist life here in the east.
So, who could deny the right to celebrate as the year turns over
and the vituperative banter of a drunken officer
shrugs off my timid request for directions in a spittle-laden retort.
So, it's another mile in the wrong direction
before bearings are properly re-established.
And as I walk I think of those whose bearings
have forever been led astray,
here at the cemetery, where candlelight vigils
create a starry night here on earth,
for all the souls to be guided
from the gravity of this life.

Zamosc, Poland
1993-1994

The Firmament of Neglect

I'm looking for a key
to the abandoned synagogue
and a diminished faith,
that's reflected
in the shattered glass
of forgetfulness and remorse.

Inquisitive neighbors
lean over crumbling ledges
in quiet amusement,
as I stumble over words,
as I stumbled over beliefs—
with my solicitous prayers directed above,
left to fend for themselves
in the firmament of neglect.

Yet, this time
a sign.
Manifest by age
in a withered hand pointing east,
towards a ramshackle garage
of coal stained men
forming metal with unrequited dreams.

These men,
who could forge a key
to any door,
laugh at my suggestion
for an entrance to God.
For they believe
I already have the key,
to everything—
being american,
being free.

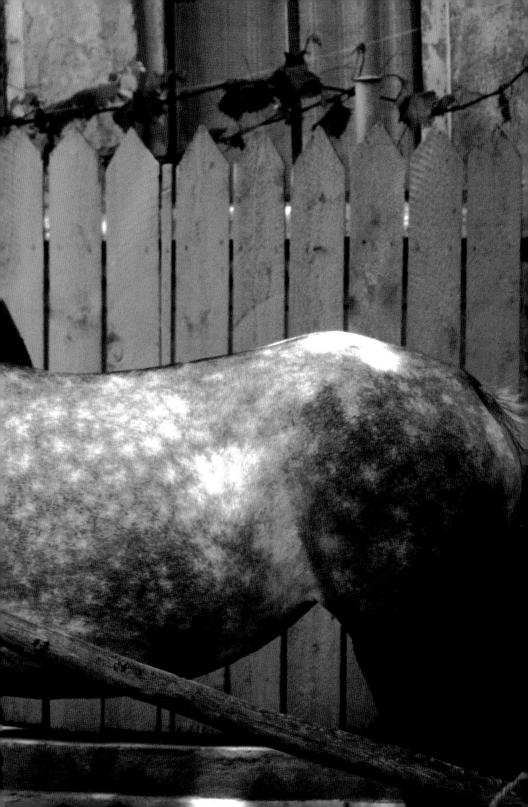

The Horseman

He never begged. Simply waved his arm in the direction of a few kids
playing in the street and mentioned that their hungry. Returning with a
bag of groceries, I pass through an old picket fence that opens onto a dirt
path. The house is a haphazard structure of rusted corrugated sheets and
weather-beaten wood. The interior is clean–meticulously clean. Eight
children are neatly arranged on the couch. Kitsch laden rugs adorn the
walls, floors and furniture. Velveteen scenes that are reminiscent of the
carpets sold off American roadsides, but with an eastern vernacular of
harlots and stallions. Sixteen eyes are riveted upon me, anxious for a meal
and the tales of a stranger. The food is quickly distributed. No one fights
or grabs from a younger sibling. British tea etiquette all the way. Only the
children eat. The adults keep to their coffee, taking pleasure in faces that
are happily chewing. A line is formed to receive the graces of chocolate,
then its back to the streets and the feral passions of youth. The horseman
thanks me and I follow his eyes as they make a tentative gesture to an
infant squirming on a bed. The child emits no sound though the arms
and legs are flaying. Gently rolling the baby over on its side, I can see the
swollen head and the disfigured spine. A father looking to me for answers.
A father in prayer for an American rescue. Feeling quite helpless, I realize
that it is too difficult to explain finality—in any language. As I make my
way to the door, the horseman thanks me once again. Sixteen eyes observe
my departure, but I'm lost in two eyes forever adrift.

Iasi, Romania
June 19, 2000

Two Women

An old woman
  reaches up to the icon.
A kiss
  planted on fingertips stretched taut.
To contact the spirit
  housed in the shrine
   outside the church
     next to the tram stop.

               ~

An old woman
  reaches into the trash.
Fingers stretched taut
  in order to sift through the bottom.
She is the last in line.
Scavenging
  what has already been cast aside.
Feeding
  on what has already fed.

Fifteen Years

Vegetables,
  freshly dug that morning
   sit upon sagging cardboard boxes.
Blackened hands shuffle the produce
  as tired voices, barely audible,
   make a plea for sales.

Urban farmers, with little to harvest
  amongst sprigs of weeds
   and tufts of grass.
Yet here they sit
  day after day.
Some, with only a meager pile of tiny potatoes,
  perched right next to someone
   with only a meager pile of tiny potatoes…

Those who are well fed speak of
" a transition period".
Postulations of time are offered
  as if this were an auction:
  ten years
   fifteen years
    two generations!

The elderly,
  who spend their days
   foraging through trash,
    aren't in on the bidding.

Journal Notes

Lunchtime in the city and platters of local delights are placed
before us, knocked down with brandy and conversation of a country
hopelessly adrift. As the discussion veers towards thoughts on
emigration, my attention is drawn to a scene outside the windows.
Several Roma families are huddled together, loading and unloading
their horse drawn carts. A scene from Dickens where filthy children
scurry about, carrying an odd assortment of scavenged urban debris.
Bearded men with haggard features adjust the reins and women
slowly shuffle along in old rayon slippers, burdened with babies and
overstuffed rucksacks. A classical portrait of futility framed in by
decrepit tenements. At least the horses can eat well, foraging in the
wild grasses of a vacant lot and I'm sure that their owners wish they
had it so easy, and as I begin to dwell on the difficult nature of this
urban existence, my gracious host call out for another round and the
dessert tray is unveiled.

Sofia, Bulgaria
May 13, 2001

Carbon-black hulks of a failed revolution stand vivid against a cerulean sky. Fields workers who make their way on trails their grandparents first carved. Onward, past newsreels, on Saturday mornings in velveteen theatres, where a few hours of imagine. But here now before me is a film in slow motion, of a ramshackle

carbon-black hulks

of golden wheat sway listlessly in the afternoon calm, unheeded by the scythe laden shattered glass of a crumbling edifice, like the bombed out cities that we viewed in darkness brought us to lands of great distance—celluloid windows we could scarcely platform brimming with workers. A procession of men tired and filthy,

of an ageless repression.

The Romanian Frontier, 2001

A Band of Gypsies

(This is not a colloquial expression)

I have already resigned myself to walking the ten miles back to town, despondent over the futility of my thumb as an instrument of roadside assistance. A parade of vehicles pass by, descending the mountain in a brash urban haste. At least there is the company of waterfalls and a forest awaking to the splendor of dusk.

An old Russian Lada pulls off onto the side of the road a short distance away. I am unsure if its broken down or actually waiting for me. I hesitate until I discern a somewhat friendly gesture of three men waving me on. I throw caution to the wind and jump in.

With a bankroll of equipment around my neck, it's difficult to be discreet about the polarity of our income brackets. The men are all smiles—like wolves I'm thinking, preparing for a feast. My fear is quickly alleviated when the driver introduces himself as the lead singer of the band, with a guitarist riding shotgun and a keyboard player beside me in the back. A genuine band of gypsies. The rolling concert commences with a beautiful folk melody. The driver has a gorgeous voice, with the physical features that would make him a teenage heartthrob anywhere else in the world. Then, as to impress his American guest, he belts out a great a cappella version of *Come Fly With Me*. The keyboard player is lightly keeping the beat on the parched, cracked vinyl. The show continues as we make our way towards the city, leaving the mountains and my worries behind.

On the outskirts of town, the driver quickly veers off to a side street at the first sign of a police barricade. These traveling troubadours, whose melodies and skills could transport them to worlds distant and welcoming, have little room to navigate through the social divide. The white men in blue have been behaving like wolves.

30

For Luminitsa

When did your dreams change? When did you begin to think that a future was possible? How long does it take to repaint the world of the soul, after so much time in the dark? Has your overcast world of no electricity, threadbare clothing and solemn expressions of defeat, finally begun to recede into the unconscious nether land of memory? Or has the spectral dance of freedom surrendered to the disparaging nature of daily life? How do we keep the world in color for you?

Detail from a poster in Bucarest commemorating the 10 year anniversary of the revolution. The government brought their Securitate army forces into the city disguised as miners to beat the protestors, students, reporters, gypsies..... Ion Iliescu ordered the assault. He was elected to the presidency in 1990, 1992 and 2000.

"I've been thinking about dying."

Today's meal
was found in the trash bin.
A bit of cake,
a morsel of cheese.
Remnants are stashed
in a worn black rucksack.
He places his faith in God's hands,
for the grip of this earthly existence
is too much to bear.
I pray that I may see him tomorrow,
even on this park bench,
even lamenting his fate.

Emerich, August 3, 2001
conversation on a park bench in Arad, Romania

Christmas in Bethlehem

Bethlehem Storefront, Dec. 24, 1995

Families on their way to the Nativity, Bethlehem, Dec. 23, 1995

Hitchhiking in the West Bank I

Trying to hitch a ride
   back to Jerusalem
Counting on
   the sheer oddity
   of my presence
   on the road
To lure some inquisitive
   good-natured soul
   into offering me a lift
Little time passes before
   an old Fiat
   chrome trim
   mag wheels
Pulls off the road
   and the door swings open
Greased black hair
   in a leather jacket
   with an upturned collar
   welcomes me in
Steel blue eyes
   and exhibiting a bit of a pouting lip
Elvis like
   or maybe James Dean
   depending on the light
A crucifix and Marilyn Monroe
   adorn the dashboard
Genuflection on the open road
He taps in the cassette
The Shondells rattle the frame
Overdrive
All the way to the border

Hevron-Jerusalem, 1995

40

First Impressions: The City of David

Over the hills and far away...
  ...busloads of tourists rumble by
  in an endless parade to the holy land.
Pilgrims,
  without peripheral vision.
Never to notice a world
  not listed in the brochure,
    where the shrieks of children
      echo across the valley.
Just some kids at play
  tossing garbage down a slope,
    to nestle in the divide
      that grows larger each year.

Journal Notes

...and so I receive a rather inquisitive look from the soldiers stationed at the corner, guarding the crossroads, where to the left, a new settlement is safely behind a barbed wire encampment. I turn right, preferring the rubble of a ghetto, or whatever they call this place, of derelict houses and dirt paths for a street, where rambunctious children frolic about in a crumbling edifice of social inequity. I immediately become the center of attention. Questions abound as to heritage and nation. Hands are thrust forward in greeting—dark, beautiful hands that are smothered in my age and paleness. A soccer ball rolls by and I instinctively give it a kick. The game commences. I throw off my pack and run wild.

A little girl in the doorway, framed in poverty but smiling non-the-less, watches her friends spin away their youth chasing down a ball through glass strewn alleyways. School's out — indefinitely. At least there is the levity of play. A mighty kick and the ball reaches up to the heavens, as do my prayers for childhood's sanctity. Especially if the child lives in the ruins of Hevron.

Hevron
Dec. 30, 1995

Journal Notes

…and so I am sitting in Mark's office at the Jerusalem Center for Public Affairs and it's my first opportunity to speak with someone who lives in a settlement out in the West Bank and he has a particularly intense fire to his eyes and in his rhetoric, describing a life built out of nothing in the desert, the only home that his children have known, and he is very forward with the issue that the land is called Judea because that is where the Jews are from and he speaks of biblical history with a certainty that makes the Bible a signed, sealed and frozen testament but I'm here to listen and he definitely has my attention when he pulls out an UZI from under the desk, explaining that he has no choice but to be armed at all times, and he tells me to take a look at his car, the one in the driveway with a broken windshield, broken by people throwing rocks this morning as he was traveling through the West Bank, taking his daughter to school, and the incident left her shaking in tears and he's now furious, espousing edicts of birthrights and land sanctioned by

God…

Jerusalem
December 21, 1995

43

Gideon

There is an expression spoken amongst the devout
that the light is twice as bright in Jerusalem.
This is for a friend who became lost in the light.

In the path of the patriarchs you so boldly followed
but the footsteps of fables are a burden to fill.
So I watched as you paced back and forth through our room
lost in the prayers of obscure incantations,
loosening the bonds of your earthly existence.

That held sway in the grip of the black gabardine,
ravenous vultures who prey on the youth,
with their deafening chorus of redemptive allure
laying claim to a soul that was no longer yours.

But I reminisce of the days spent cascading on bikes
through Herod's old haunt and where David once reigned,
singing our songs of celebration and might,
bonding our lives with the land and the light,
that wove through our studies, our thoughts and debates
towards a virtuous life we'd never attain.

So Gideon my friend,
your namesake of heroes and battles of old,
recited in stories we learned of on Sundays,
was defenseless against your insufferable doubts
about spirit and souls and a kingdom to come.
But I hear you're now safe in the comforts of care,
where the radiance of God is now distilled down to this —
institutional white lights and soft prayers in the night.

Jerusalem '93

They shot a man today
  right by the wall
All traces of blood
  quickly removed
From ancient stones
  soaked in blood

Christmas in Bethlehem.

The Israeli government is in the process of transferring governance of the city over to the Palestinian Authority. The milieu is one of great anticipation laced with hope and promises for a new independence. Combat boots and automatic weapons are the fashion of the day. The colors of the pageantry are formed by a whirlwind of militia in vibrant red berets, policemen in blue uniforms and thousands of plastic flags streaming overhead. Waves of buses converge on the main square and the pilgrims disembark — holiday pilgrims in matching hats and buttons that announce, *I'm from Dallas*. They are greeted by a thirty-foot banner emblazoned with the image of Arafat — hand drawn by the FATAH Arts Committee. Welcome to the West Bank.

Bethlehem
Dec. 23, 1995

مرحبا بالقائد الرمز

اللجنة
الحركية
العليا
فتح

اقليم

بيت لحم

قيادة وكوادر واعضاء

Fatah
Welcomes
The President
Arafat

& SCULPTURE
GIACAMAN & SONS CO.

OLIVE WOOD
FACTORY
P.O.BOX 230 TEL./FAX 742837

MOTHER OF PEARL & OLIVE WOOD
HAND CARVING

HOLY LAND A
GIACAMAN B

Bethlehem, Dec. 23, 1995

Journal Notes: Interview with Ali Jeddah

Navigating the streets of East Jerusalem, it is easy to become lost amongst the side alleys and the lack of directional information. We enter several buildings before we arrive at our destination — The Palestine Human Rights Organization, where a viewing window opens and piercing eyes look down upon us. A buzzer sounds, the door swings open and Ali Jeddah fills the frame. He greets us with indifference and we follow him through the office to his little cubicle. He has distinctive African features and speaks English with a refined accent. Three chairs and a desk fill the space as we sit close together.

I promised to be a wallflower during the interview so Rebecca asks the questions — political in nature. Their dialogue follows the topical issues of the day and a quiet tension begins to fill the air. There isn't much in the way of acquiescence to disparate beliefs, from either side. After twenty minutes, Rebecca has heard enough and clicks off the tape recorder. I hesitantly inquire of Ali Jeddah if I may ask him a few questions (even wallflowers need occasional watering). He nods in agreement.

How many kids do you have?
The tension in the room is quickly alleviated as Ali Jeddah takes on the glow of a proud father. Names and ages and personality types are boisterously expounded upon. He addresses the difficulty of raising children in a hostile environment and laments the condition of the schools and the educational system. At this point, the conversation veers towards perspectives for social change. Ali Jeddah speaks slowly and clearly:

"I believe that we must achieve our goals as Palestinians through peaceful objectives. But I also believe, that the terrorists acts of the PLO during 1968-1973 were necessary in order to establish who we are." (Ali Jeddah spent several years in prison for terrorist activities in Israel. He was released during the Syrian prisoner exchange.)

I glance over to Rebecca whose rage is obvious, thank Ali Jeddah for his time and request a picture of him at his desk. He smiles. A logo for The Palestine Human Rights Organization flashes across the computer screen.

East Jerusalem, Dec. 20, 1995

48

Crayons

Flags of statehood hover above — colors of a new identity forming a rainbow of optimism, dressing up this urban blight of dilapidated buildings with crumbling stairwells, where broken pipes leach ferrous water onto leaden paint walls. In the damp office of the Ministry of Culture I am warmly received by the Director of Children's Theatre. A woman of solemn principles, she is responsible for staging dramas on a stage already dramatic. Behind her desk there are a series of drawings pinned up on the wall. Childlike renderings in crayon of expressionistic figures in muted tones. She bids me to closer inspection. A man is bound, tied to a chair, head askew, beaten. The signature at the bottom is the confident gesture of her eight-year-old son. My obvious disbelief — her resolute response: *the children know.*

I'm left to wonder — will this child ever be capable of drawing a house, with a lemon tree in the garden? Will this child ever have a reason to draw a flower, a blazing yellow sun, shedding light on the green, green grass?

Ramallah
Dec.17, 1995

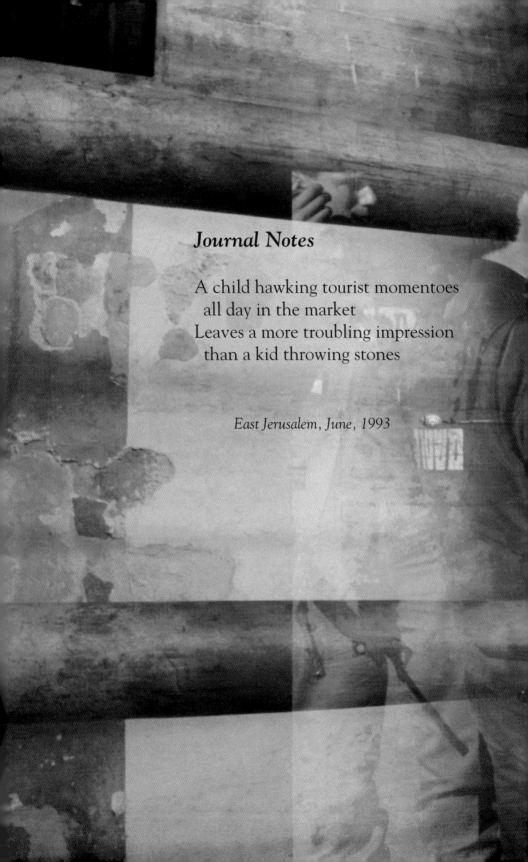

Journal Notes

A child hawking tourist momentoes
   all day in the market
Leaves a more troubling impression
   than a kid throwing stones

East Jerusalem, June, 1993

Ramallah Redux

Great sadness descends upon me as I catch a glimpse of the day's events in the West Bank. The airport monitor reveals images that have become all too familiar. A group of Palestinian men are rolling a car towards a barricade, stones are thrown, the Israeli's shoot and the story goes on. Ramallah is in complete upheaval – again.

My dismay springs forth from the hope that I once experienced there – during a much different time. In a place that is now unrecognizable. The winter of '95 brought the first implementation of the Oslo Peace Accords as the city of Ramallah was granted it's sovereignty. The people radiated with optimism, fully aware that their future was now in their hands. I felt to be walking through a new chapter in history, breathing the pages as the people willed them to be written. A gentleman in a suit stood before me, his hand held out in a gesture of welcome, thanking me for visiting his town. The market place was bustling, an air of exuberance filled the stalls as street vendors readied their wares for the coming day. Businessmen were gathered in cafes, chain-smoking their way through spontaneous sessions on urban renewal. The sky was a rainbow of independence as thousands of flags set claim to the territory. Children ran by, wrapped in this new identity, looking like little superheroes with liberty's cape trailing behind.

Six years hence and the capes have become shrouds, adorning the coffins that are passed along the funerary march. The schools are closed, the borders are sealed and the economy is in ruins. The promise of statehood has all but diminished, and the yellow flags of Hezbollah now accompany the rainbow of independence. As the news rolls on I look for the man who welcomed me to his town, his city of Ramallah. Possibly he is there, in amongst the fighting and chaos, trying to reclaim a sense of the future.

Wyoming, 2001

Hitchhiking in the West Bank II

The man in the front seat turns around to get a good look at the stranger, raises up his arm, forming the shape of a gun with his hand, points it at his head and begins bantering me in Arabic. He's smiling all the while, an unnerving smile that breaks into laughter, as his mock gun waves in the air and I discern a trickle of sweat breaking out over my whole body and I'm starting to feel like a kosher sandwich pressed into the backseat with several Palestinians who are now all staring at me, nodding their heads in agreement and laughing along with my tormentor and the sweat is pouring as the loaded finger is now pointed at my head and when I'm at the point where there is no sense in trying to conceal the extreme paranoia that is gripping my bones the gentleman sitting next to me inquires, in perfect London educated English, *We want to know if you have a gun.* Flaying my arms wildly and yelling *American artist, American artist,* the whole carload of accomplices breaks out in laughter, and we continue onwards, safely to the border.

Bethlehem-Jerusalem, 1995

A Quiet Divide

Here by the border, there is a restless peace, a quiet divide.
How long before the noise of disintegration begins?

Kishtani, Macedonia, July 2001

Return to the Land of Alexander

We're begging the driver to slow down. He waves off the suggestion and proceeds headlong into a flock of birds. There is a momentary angelic blur before the sickening crack of death hits the windshield. Sensing our outrage, he smiles and holds up two fingers to imply that he killed only two birds. I grab hold of the dashboard, and softly whisper a prayer for deliverance.

It is June 26th, and the United Sates is evacuating all non-essential personnel from Macedonia. We received assurances from our friends that a south-westerly route across the country was safe and that we wouldn't encounter any difficulties. Coming from Blagoevgrad, Bulgaria, the road to the border is a beautiful ascent through meadows and pine forests. The crossing sits at the precipice of a mountain range, where the peaceful solitude of two countries can be breathtaking — and deceptive.

The border is quiet and the guards are lounging about with their coffee. Their surprised to have foreigners *entering* their country so we're bombarded with questions. Inquiries of politics are soon forgotten when they discover the camera gear in the bags. In typical Balkan fashion, the guards want to know how much it costs, where they can buy it for less, and what are my thoughts on the digital age. We cross over with ease, receiving their blessings for a safe journey.

The view is glorious and the air is clear. We strap on the bags and begin our descent. The emotional charge of being back in Macedonia serves us well for hiking the first few miles — then it gets hot. Real hot, and the pleasures of return are quickly diminished. The sound of a tractor emerging from a field brings anticipation, so we stick out our thumbs and hope for the best. Within a few minutes, the packs are strapped onto the engine cover and we're riding shotgun on the wheel wells. We cruise for several miles in relative comfort to a village on the outskirts of Delchevo. The calloused hands of a farmer swallow my grip of gratitude and we continue on our way.

Reaching the main boulevard we are verbally accosted by a group of young men, their shirts off and waiving rifles in the air — boasting like roosters. We didn't take it personally. Their outrage was against American policy. The previous week, the American military intervened in the conflict by rounding up the Albanian insurgents, placing them on buses and driving them back to Kossovo — with their weapons intact.

The milieu of Delchevo is more accurately reflected in the somber expression of a man waiting for transit. He is dressed in a new uniform, an artillery jacket slung over the shoulder and a box of new combat boots tucked under the arm. The situation was too graven for boasting.

At the bus station word gets out that Americans have arrived. Within fifteen minutes we are surrounded — by the Advanced English class from the local high school. The kids are humorous and intelligent, possessing grammatical skills well beyond my American vernacular. Here, there is no talk of war. Only questions about college, entrance exams and scholarships. Surrounded by these precocious kids, the future of Macedonia begins to look enlightened and peaceful. Well may it last.

Delchevo, Macedonia
June 26th, 2001

A Day in the Life of Father Kliment

"I have never seen the angles.
Only the devil, and he looked like me."

The Zrze Monastery is emblematic of Macedonia's return to its spiritual
heritage. Barren and left to fester during the socialist reign, it is now
populated with ten monks, a crew of laborers, a dizzying array of
scaffolding, and several cats. Renovations are being funded through the
central government and the man responsible for all of this activity is
Archimandrit (Father) Kliment. Sitting in the garden, conversing over
cucumber sandwiches, Father Kliment strikes a traditional pose of religious
authority – a long black beard, flowing robes and a smile that welcomes
you to the table. He relishes a rigorous debate, challenging his guests on
questions of metaphysics and the soul.

At the age of thirty he is already highly esteemed and established within
the hierarchy of the Orthodox Church. He received "the calling" at age
seven, and by ten he was rigorously studying the Bible. As to be expected,
his determination caused significant anguish and worry for his parents who
dreamed of their highly precocious son ascending to the presidency of the
country. His father had an oft-repeated expression–*be everything, but not a*
monk. After spending two years on Mt. Athos his mother finally relented
when she understood his determination. His grandmother, on the other
hand, was overjoyed to have a priest in the family. This is not an unusual
scenario. In Macedonia, there is a convergence of three generations, each
with a distinctive religious history. The elders experienced the tenets of
faith and their renouncement, the middle generation never had access to
the church, and the late-Tito/post-Tito generation could listen to the bell
towers once again ring the call to prayer. A young child heeded the call.

"The mind has frontiers, not the spirit."

From the garden, we have a view of the caves that the first ascetics
inhabited. Dark holes that seem to parallel Father Kliment's beliefs in the
darkness–a place of morbid tragedy and spiritual pain that prepares the
soul for the light. He speaks of his visitation, followed by two weeks of
physical illness and spiritual drowning. He declares that we must listen to

the source and to name this source. We question the necessity of naming the mystery. We argue that a name leads to disfranchisement and division. He declares *Christos*. We declare *the light*. We all turn to the sky.

Standing before the alter, surrounded by 14th century frescoes, he allows his voice to slowly rise, merging with the light and our visions of angels. Time disconnects. We are here to receive. Afterwards, we thank him for the beautiful song. He reminds us that the chant is not for us. It is *"for the mother of God"*.

"There will be a war."

As daylight turns to dusk, we are perched on the rocks, looking out over the valley. It's a stunning panorama of ancient villages and sloping fields of grain. Father Kliment speaks about the conflict in a resigned manner. He has been personally chastised and rebuked by the local media for his kindness to Albanians. We discuss the fate of the monasteries in the west and his reply underlies his faith – *"God will choose"*.

He walks us to the gate and waives goodbye as we journey down the mountain. His voice resonates a clear deep tone through the mountain air:

"Everyone is a monk. Everyone is one."

Zrze-Prilep, Macedonia
June 29, 2001

The Call to Arms

Krushevo, Macedonia, July 2001

Evgenia's husband —

What becomes of a country when a father with a newborn child requests permission to fight? With the economy in ruins, and little hope of finding work in this small village, the war has brought employment. Enlisted to night patrol, he is overjoyed at his new prosperity. A prolonged conflict will provide a steady income. He now sets his sights on the front – a significant raise if he can get in on the action. Daily appeals for a transfer go unheeded. In a nation of reluctant warriors he is ready and willing. This is not about battle or glory–merely a father who has lost his way. War has become a reprieve, casting aside years of shame when he was unable to support a family. This is a traditional land, and the stature of responsibility is still a workingman's claim. Now, as a proud soldier, he stands on the corner with an automatic by his side, gently rocking the baby carriage, idly goggling at his three-month-old son.

Dragan Ristov, journalist —

I love my country. I would go and fight immediately.
But someone has to tell me what we are fighting for.

Rade's wife —

Burjana dabs at her eyes as she becomes absorbed in the photo album. There is a faded, yellow image of her brother, who long ago left for America and never returned. In this house, there are no conversations about the war. Enough lives have been lost.

Sasho Bokovski, Lieutenant in the Macedonian Army —

This war isn't fair.

Bibi Petreski, student —

Last night I dreamed of my father. Three men were standing outside our house. They were holding a platter with my father's head upon it.
This morning, three men came to our home. They handed my father his military orders. My father didn't even bother to read the paper. They all marched off together.

"I never thought that there would be another war here."

Sitting at the kitchen table, stories and intrigues
unencumbered by time slowly make their way across an old
map of Yugoslavia. Her husband's war medals are close at
hand, housed in a plastic jewelry case upon the shelf.
A humble man, he still travels to Belgrade to receive
treatments for a wound suffered in battle. A large picture
of Tito is prominently displayed next to family portraits and
wedding snapshots. There is a genuine affection and
nostalgia towards a country they were willing to
fight for — ideals that no longer exist.

*Violeta Yovanoska, photographed in 1944 while serving
as a partisan fighter for Josip Broz. Struga, Macedonia, July 2001*

three figures on a couch
awash in the melancholy blue haze
of late night broadcasts

channel surfing
for news from the front

Prilep, Macedonia, June, 2001

Vevchani:

Excerpts From Market Day, July 2001

*As the war in northern Macedonia was cutting a sharp division in the politics,
culture and geography of the country, there were still regions in the south where
communities of Macedonians and ethnic Albanians continued to work together
and live in peace. Vevchani is a small Macedonian village outside of Struga.
Thursday is market day, when hundreds of ethnic Albanian and Macedonian
people are gathered together in the village square, to buy and sell produce, and
to rekindle friendships. This is the Macedonia that I remember from stories.
This is the Macedonia that nourishes the soul.*

I am an old fool, professes the man under the tree, shaded from the sun and
the still harsher news of the day. He is holding court with friends by his
side. He directs me to listen to the youth in the streets, yet he continues
to speak—espousing his thoughts of identity and history, his concerns
over war and the abyss of forgetfulness. He continues to speak,
in order to remember.

~

Two men in a café
  sit shoulder to shoulder
  as their fathers did before them
Lamenting the lunacy of politicians
  as they toast forty years of a friendship
  not recognized in the north
Calling forth to all strangers
  to join them in drink
  and celebrate the union of this national treasure

~

Florina smiles and reaches deep within the layers of her brightly colored
garments to unveil a worn, yellowed piece of paper. A government
document with stamps and signatures from 1969, officially providing
this market stall to her family. Over thirty years in this spot, feeding the
village and the ravenous birds. She forcefully pulls off my backpack and
fills me up with produce and stories.

In Memory of Dr. Dejanov

The truth will always survive generation to generation.
I don't have fifteen years to chase philosophy. We'll keep things simple.
A peace center to educate and publish. To forgive. To never forget.
To reorient people towards making a contribution to society.
To relearn how to love, and leave the hate behind.
                    Dr. Ivan Dejanov, Skopje, Macedonia 1998

He never mentioned that he was dying of cancer. He still had too much to accomplish, too many memories to rescue. As the initiator and driving force behind the Macedonian Holocaust Memorial Center in Skopje, his days were filled with meetings, planning and strategy. He retired from his medical practice in order to devote the rest of his life to his dream of rebuilding a Jewish community. The architectural plans for the Center detailed a library, a publishing house and a memorial. Dr. Dejanov carried an unbridled enthusiasm for the project. Earlier in the year, Kiro Gligorov, the President of Macedonia, unveiled a small memorial that designated a site along the banks of the Vardar river as the future home for the Macedonian Holocaust Memorial Center. The memorial recounts the Day of Deportation, March 11, 1943, when the Macedonian Jews were deported to Treblinka. Those who survived the harrowing journey in the sealed train cars were immediately gassed upon arrival.

There are no physical traces remaining of the old Jewish Quarter in Skopje. As we walked along the banks of the Vardar river, Dr. Dejanov unfolded the rich tapestry of Jewish history in Macedonia, speaking slowly and willing us to gaze across the waters and visualize–the houses, the market, the Jewish Little Bridge, the people. We discussed the idea of recreating the Jewish Little Bridge, even in a metaphorical context, as a means of linking time and memory – as a means of linking a new community to the old.

Dr. Dejanov's enthusiasm stood in sharp contrast to his partner's pessimism. Dr. Samuel Sadikaro is also a highly distinguished research physician in Macedonia. He recently co-authored a significant work on anti-Semitism, focusing on the difficulties faced by Jewish communities throughout the Balkans. He too is immersed in the resuscitation of memory – he was raised by a Holocaust survivor.

Although Dr. Sadikario passionately believes in the necessity of the Macedonian Holocaust Memorial Center for teaching and remembrance, he does not feel that the center will serve as a catalyst for rebuilding a Jewish community. He feels that Macedonia, with its current political and social malaise is ill equipped to redevelop a cultural and educational infrastructure that could support a burgeoning Jewish community. The current Macedonian Jewish populace numbers in the low hundreds. In the early part of the twentieth century, there were approximately ten thousand Jews living in Macedonia.

The sense of entropy in this endeavor seemed overbearing. Dr. Dejanov's health was waning and a conflict between the ethnic Albanians and the Macedonians appeared inevitable. Still, they marched on together along the banks of the Vardar, facing uncertainty but confronting a dream – a dream of remembrance.

For Dushan

When his children ask
  where he lived
  where he played
  where was grandma's house
How can he possibly explain
  the disappearance
Of ancient stone bridges and cobbled streets
Of ice cream dripping on Sunday clothes
  in forested parks with bell towers distant
How can he possibly explain
  nothingness
To youthful eyes
  of splendid innocence

Milam Petrovic, Belgrade, 2001

Belgrade Street Corner

In front of the local tavern
a robust woman stands on the corner
displaying a hearty disposition and a toothless smile.
She senses an American in her presence
which commences a flurry of hand gestures
as a prelude to speech.
I anticipate a verbal assault,
a diatribe of political protestations
or at the very least,
a reprimand.
Instead,
two little words —
Clinton and bombs.
She bellows with laughter.

77 Nights: A Bedtime Rhyme

1.

Portentous skies
of an ominous front
Recall grievous tales
of American brunt
Not rain nor lightening
was the nemesis then
But cluster bombs
and a fear without end

A walk in the morning
muffled prayers from within
To spy out the damage
to LIVE once again
To wake each day
with children at hand
Impossible to explain
the reason/a plan

I remember those days
as surely should you
For now we are gathered
to break bread and renew
With glasses we toast
the friendship and wine
But a storm once again
has entered our lives
Real rain this time
not a thunderous disguise
Still we gather round the table
with traditional delights
A Belgrade home
A Serbian night

2.

Rain slaps hard
in a hastening rhythm
Howling winds
hush conversation
Momentary darkness
proceeds the thunder
A deafening roar
like a night demon's plunder
A young child screams
from memories of planes
Seeks the warmth of his mother
the shelter he claims
The percussion of bombs
still needs consoling
A rumble of childhood
still needs explaining

Balkan Express

My journey into
the Balkans has fortuitous
beginnings as I open the sleeping
compartment and discover a woman
with a small child occupying the lower
berth. Introductions are made in English and
I notice that the little boy is reading a Superman
comic. Speaking in Serbian, I ask him about his hero.
The mother's astonished expression provides me with the
nerve to slip in a simple question to her—"how is life in Belgrade?"
Roll the tape.
I could not write fast enough. I was the gracious recipient of a whirlwind
tour of geography, history, socio-economic conditions, and of course, the
contentious issue of US foreign policy. Kossovo is repeated as in a dirge.
Only the train conductor can derail her thoughts. For here on the frontier,
a Serbian passport is still persona non grata.

Hungarian Countryside, 1998

The Nightly News

The factory in Prilep still has several posters of Tito adorning the walls, where workers can reminisce about salaries and red meat. Coffee, cigarettes, and an occasional task at the lathe churn away the hours for these men. After work we would take our places at the bar and turn our attention towards the nightly news. Several months prior to the "official recognition" that a war was occurring in Kossovo, we would watch the daily bombardment from the secure confines of our hotel watering hole. We discovered later that the television coverage we were viewing was not being broadcast overseas. Priorities, I guess. Smoke filled valleys and Serbian tanks. Bombed out homes and a trail of refugees. After the newscast on a particularly brutal day of fighting, everyone in the bar glanced over to Dushan, our lone Yugoslavian representative for a word of explanation (or at the very least, a morsel of clarity). His bewildered expression along with a shrug of the shoulders and upturned palms had us all roaring with laughter.
Who can explain any of this?

Prilep, Macedonia
July, 1998

First Impressions: *Albania*

The border is within shouting distance.
For some time now
I have been listening patiently
   to the accusations:

Overpopulation
   Over breeding
      Uneducated peasants
         Talk of a revolution
            They will outnumber us
               An intentional plan
                  Muslim!

The hostility of the condemnations
   has an inverse effect upon me,
for I am drawn increasingly closer
   towards the people in question.
And where others perceive confrontation,
I discover
   the beauty of a sleeping child.

Struga, Macedonia, August, 1998

Last Thoughts On Macedonia

I telephoned Djevat from the airport to say goodbye and to offer one last prayer for his family in Kumanovo. I carry with me an image of his three sisters, huddled in the den, listening to mortar fire and watching the broadcasts of nearby battles. An Albanian adrift in the west, he finds consolation in his small community of friends, where gathered for lunch they can dine on memories and recent news from the front. Djevat and I met by chance, sharing a seat on the metro (although I really can't think of this as anything but fortuitous). As strangers on a train, we were careful with our words to one another — for these are heady times to be professing truths. By the time we ordered drinks we became spirited combatants discussing culture, civil rights and history. By closing we had resolved nothing, but had begun a friendship. May his country be so fortunate.

Vienna, 2001

Albanian bride, Struga Macedonia, July, 2001

Ground Cover

The New Jewish Cemetary, Krakow, Poland, 1993

Nature will traverse its unbiased path
and stories shall become our only alliance
in the persistence of memory.

The footprints I leave behind in the snow are the only remnants of a Jewish identity. Below, the Vistula river, once the carriage of trade has long since forgotten the parting waves of the merchant ships. The beauty of this panoramic vista is shrouded by the absence of a people and the suppression of memory. There will be no postcard images on this day.

Kazmierz Dolny, Poland, Dec., 1993

The negative pall
cast upon this place
cannot remove
my sense of homecoming.

Eternal grey
leaves no shadow
In footprints
dragged through winter's blight

Janowiec, Poland, 1993

Balkan Summer

Balkan Summer

Patience,
and letting go
  of time,
    schedules and appointments.
To breathe and recognize
the significance of each day,
  gently illuminating
    the dark hollows of memory.

As a walk after lunch
brings a flutter of wings,
  like hovering angels
    at play in the breeze.
For breadcrumbs gifts
from a joyous old woman,
  conversant with birds
    perched on her shoulder.

A window ledge queen
holding court at three storeys,
  casting alms across rooftops
    of ancient clay tiles.
That stretch to the shores
of secretive rivers,
  defining this city
    while yearning for sea.

Singeorz-Bai, Romania, 2001

Singeorz-Bai

Waves of color splash across a woman's back
   in a woolen rainbow that reaches into the generations
Of mountain hamlet characters and fabled eccentrics
   whose tales are still embellished by whiskey-laden men
Gathered on the porch to soften the hours
   absorbing the glow of the day's brief warmth
That will not return until the late morning sun
   washes over the market and ancient dirt roads
Where adolescent girls are bundled in gossip
   and the stretch polyester of a nouveau chic look
That compresses a cycle of traditional yarns
   from woman to daughter to woman to daughter.

Singeorz-Bai, Romania, 2001

Tonel Schlessinger and the Jews of Arad, Romania

I have been to the west. Twice. What's the big deal? Money isn't everything. Here, I can be of service. Here, I can be Romanian.

The President of the Jewish Community of Arad, Romania welcomes me into his office. We sit together on the couch. He takes his time to look me over. Finally, he begins to speak, asking me if I am Jewish. I nod my head in agreement. He laughs and mentions, *well, nobody's perfect.*

Tonel's humor serves him well in his battle with entropy. As the overseer of the Jewish community he maintains a passionate and spirited watch over the declining populace. Those who had the financial and/or physical capabilities to emigrate have left, leaving behind an elderly, infirmed community. The Jewish Care Home is housed in an old building that has served the Jewish populace for many years. During the Communist era, when study of the Torah was prohibited, this building contained a secret passage into a room that served as a yeshiva. The synagogue was closed but the people maintained their identity, their prayer and their community. Today, with financial assistance from the west, the synagogue can once again open its doors to celebrate and cherish Arad's cultural history. In 2000, *Sixty Minutes* filmed a feature story here. Afterwards, donations began to pour in, providing the much needed maintenance and repairs. The bookkeeper mentions her disappointment that donations have slowly trailed off and there is still so much left to be done.

The Care Home maintains a dining hall — a large chandeliered ballroom with elegant drapery and seating for forty. Sadly, only about ten people are capable of taking their meals in the dining hall. The kitchen services about seventy people, most of whom are infirm, residing at the Care Home or in their own apartments. A network of individuals helps distribute the meals, looks in on the elderly and provides some companionship. Proud to be kosher and very well humored, the kitchen crew are not deterred by the small appetites of the aged residents. The counters are clean, the floor is well mopped and there is enough soup, goulash and fried chicken for everyone. I am force-fed a sample of everything.

Stephan's smile is contagious. As a volunteer caregiver for over a decade, he imparts tenderness and love on a daily basis. A dental assistant by trade, he accepts life as it is: *During the war, our lives were saved by the Russians. Later, we learned what it meant to be **saved** by the Russians. My father tried to immigrate to Israel twice during the 1950's. Our family sold everything, applied for the appropriate papers, and at the last minute we were turned away. All we ever received was a short letter stating that we were refused permission to leave Romania. In 1988, my brother finally moved to Israel with his wife. He loves it there, but he feels that the move came a bit too late in life.* Stephan folds his hands and makes a gesture of bringing his feet down hard onto the floor: *I'm Romanian, I'm grounded here.*

The elderly are grounded in remembrance. Although I intentionally avoid any questions pertaining to the war, the subject is inevitably brought up in their conversation. As they speak, tears well up in their eyes and the stories of spouses, deportations and a life of isolation fill the dining hall:

Miss Hershfield sheds tears for a daughter who passed away from heart failure at the tender age of twenty-eight. She decries that a mother should never have to experience her own daughter's funeral.

Rosa is a spirited and highly animated woman who at ninety-two appears to have another decade ahead of her. She jokes about her tablemate's voracious eating habits and the gossipy nature of the lunchroom. As soon as she begins to speak of her departed husband she turns away, her eyes brimming with tears. She bemoans the length of each day, the hours passed without her soul mate.

Agnes is a pillar of culture, elegantly dressed for any occasion. We sit with her for an hour listening to family histories and tales. Educated in all things French, she is passionate about her life and travels to Israel and France. She staggers a bit in her speech as she begins to recount her husband. She is still troubled by her decision not to move to America when they had the opportunity. Her husband was very much in favor of leaving. Then they got stuck here, closed in, as did so many others.

A woman who has been quietly sitting with us at the table speaks up suddenly: *I want out, hopefully to Israel.* She is one of the care workers who assist in the distribution of money and food to the elderly residents, along with providing friendship. She will be dearly missed.
As will all of these gentle souls for whom life is slowly receding–
the Jews of Arad, Romania.

Maria, Vitolishte, Macedonia, 1998

Forty Years

Slowly becoming
the man I set out to be.
I had no idea
it would take this long.

Koprivshtitsa, Bulgaria
June 10, 2001

Journal Notes: Robert Bly For A Day

I introduce myself to Paskal Gilevski, Director of the Struga Poetry Evenings and his enthusiasm strikes me as a bit odd. After all, I am just one of the thousand or so folks attending the festival, where writers recite their works on the Bridge of Poets, casting out poems to the sacred waters of Lake Ochrid. Paskal takes me by the arm and leads me into a room with long tables and a row of typewriters along the wall. Speaking through an interpreter he inquires if I can write something for him. I explain that I am here only as a lover of poetry. He presses on–"*…can't you write me something, a short essay. Something on American poetry."* I try to explain again that I am really a sculptor who enjoys writing highly personal journal based stories. *"No problem"*, he responds. *"I need only a short* **speech**, *maybe five minutes long. You will present it tomorrow at the conference during the session on Poetry of the 20th Century."*

I'm beginning to wonder if were having translation difficulties. The interpreter smiles and confirms that everything is okay. I make one last attempt to explain myself to Paskal: *"Paskal, I really like poetry. I have even written a few short poems, but it's been fifteen years since I have been in an English lit class that barely skimmed over a few notable works."* Paskal shakes his head and smiles: *"No problem. The American poet just called and he had to cancel his appearance at the festival. And your American."* (I was the *only* American in town).

I ask Paskal who was going to attend the festival. He grabs my pen and writes out Robert Bly. He hands back my pen, smiles and mentions, *"Your panel discussion is tomorrow at 1:00pm. See you then."* I glance over at the typewriters. Its going to be a long night.

Struga, Macedonia, Aug. 21, 1998

Writers perform their works on the Bridge of Poets
during the grand finale of "Struga Poetry Evenings"

Struga, Macedonia, 1998

St. Marko

When I close my eyes I can still hear the bells of the goats. Each morning
I awoke with an urgency to return to the mountain. The crash of the horns
and the ringing of bells became a mantra—a spectral dance that called
me forth to an age that hasn't slipped away. I would perch myself upon a
ledge, mesmerized, as battles were played out for command of the herd.
The shepherds would lean upon their walking sticks, keeping watch with a
distant yet thoughtful gaze, as their grandfathers did before them, as their
grandfathers…

Occasionally, they would gather into a circle to exchange their daily banter, punctuating words with a forceful jab of a cane into the dust. Ancient smiles and exuberant gestures defined their character. Over time, they became accustomed to my presence, eventually including me in their conversations. Cheerful and inquisitive, they wanted to learn about America while I yearned to hear of their world. There was never enough time, nor enough words to fully immerse myself into their ancestral lives. I reminisce of them still, perched on their mountain, quietly following a dream that cannot be swept away by the tides of history.

St. Marko Mountain, Prilep, Macedonia, 1998

I wonder,
how many children here grow up
dreaming of departure,
to frolic in the diesel and dust
and disco cacophony of the cities.
And how many arrive at maturity
comfortable
and at peace here in the mountains.
Where a spiritual life is recovered
in the ritual of daily chores
and a meditative glance
into this spectacular landscape,
listening to one's breath
in sync with the world.

Monastir, Bulgaria, June 13, 2001

Departure

I am here
because I missed the train
from Budapest to Oradea.

I am here
because I forgot
to set my watch ahead
and missed the train
from Arad to Oradea.

I am still here
because
my heart says stay.

Arad, Romania
August 1, 2001

Ancient Croatian Manuscript, Rijeka Library and Modern Art Museum

Constantine's father, Putna, Romania, 2000

About the Author

Roger Colombik lives in the Texas Hill Country with his wife Jerolyn, two dogs and around thirty chickens depending on the appetite of the hawks, foxes, racoons. As a professional artist over the past eighteen years he has been involved in a number of projects that have been visually engaging and conceptually diverse. Large-scale public sculptures, DVD based installations and documentary photography attempt to create visual environments that soften the flight of time for the viewer. He is currently working on a book of photographs and essays based upon his experiences in the Republic of Georgia — where the beautiful traditions of an ancient culture confront the harsh realities of the post-Soviet hangover. His online portfolio can be viewed at www.colombikart.com.

Jean -
Thanks for your support
over the years.
Best Wishes
ROGER
2006